THIS BOOK BELONGS TO

For Gus – LB
For Madeleine, Theo and Freddie – RLO

First published in Great Britain 2021 by Farshore
An imprint of HarperCollins*Publishers*
1 London Bridge Street, London SE1 9GF

farshore.co.uk

HarperCollins*Publishers*
1st Floor, Watermarque Building, Ringsend Road
Dublin 4, Ireland

ISBN 978 0 0085 0292 8
Printed and bound in Australia by McPhersons Printing Group
1

A CIP catalogue record for this title is available from the British Library.

THE NAUGHTIEST UNICORN

ON A TREASURE HUNT

PIP BIRD

ILLUSTRATED BY DAVID O'CONNELL

Farshore

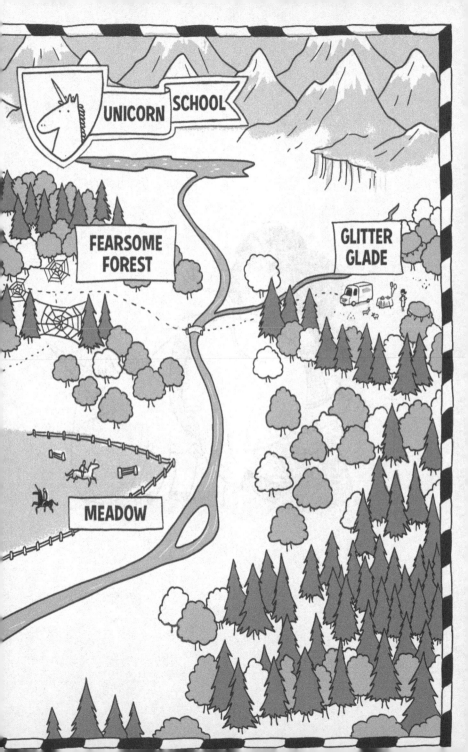

Contents

CHAPTER ONE
Searching for Special Treasure...

'Unicorns ready?' said Miss Glitterhorn, sleepily.

The unicorns neighed and stamped their hooves.

'Unicorn school students ready?' said the teacher, stifling a yawn.

'YES!!' yelled Mira along with the rest of Class Red.

Mira and her classmates had all got up super early and come to the pumpkin patch in the Unicorn School grounds. It was the

Longest Day of the Year, and they were going to watch the sunrise. Everyone was excited about it. Everyone, that is, except for Mira's unicorn, Dave, who was still very much asleep. Mira had had to drag him here by his hooves with the help of her best friends Raheem and Darcy and their unicorns. For a small unicorn, Dave was surprisingly heavy.

'Dave!' Mira whispered excitedly. 'Wake up! It's nearly sunrise!'

Dave stretched in his sleep and let out an almighty sleepfart, which echoed around the pumpkin patch like a thunderclap. Some of the unicorns whinnied in alarm and a flock of birds flew out from one of the trees.

Mira shrugged. At least Dave's bum was awake, even if the rest of him wasn't.

Dave wasn't like the other unicorns at Unicorn School. They were all sparkly and elegant and did what they were told, like getting up early for the Longest Day Sunrise.

Dave, on the other hoof, was grumpy and greedy and rarely did what he was told, unless what he was being told to do was eat seventeen doughnuts in a row or do a poo the size of his own head. But he was Mira's UBFF (Unicorn Best Friend Forever) and having fun adventures with him was her favourite thing in the world.

'I see the sunrise!' yelled Tamsin.

Mira saw that rays of light were beginning to break through the clouds on the horizon. Everyone popped their sunglasses on, careful not to look directly at the sun, then they watched as it began to peep over the edge of the Crystal Mountains. The sky was lit up

purple and pink and then orange as the sun
glimmered over the mountain top, giving out
more sparkly rays. The children oohed and
aahed and did a few yawns because it really
was very early. The unicorns clapped their
hooves and Dave did another sleepfart.

'Right, Class Red,' said Miss Glitterhorn. 'It's
time to have some fun testing your unicorns'
treasure hunting skills!'

A month before, all the unicorns had
buried a carrot somewhere in the patch,
and now they were going to dig them up.
Miss Glitterhorn had promised there would
be a PRIZE for the first unicorn to find the
treasure. The prize was the bit Mira and her

friends were most excited about!

Mira gave her sleeping unicorn a big nudge. He would want to be awake for this! But Dave just rolled over and did an extra-loud snore.

'Now the sunrise carrot dig is an important Longest Day of the Year tradition,' said Miss Glitterhorn. 'I remember doing it when I was at Unicorn School!'

'A hundred years ago?' said Flo in amazement.

'Not quite,' said Miss Glitterhorn with a frown. 'Anyway, we always start the Longest Day with the carrot dig to prepare the unicorns for all the treasure hunting that is to come.'

'Pegasus was BORN prepared,' said Jake, patting his unicorn on the neck. Pegasus snorted confidently.

'You might not know that unicorns have a special ability to remember where they bury things,' continued Miss Glitterhorn.

'Like squirrels?' asked Seb.

'But more magical,' said Tamsin.

'Exactly,' said Miss Glitterhorn. 'So the first activity of the Longest Day shouldn't actually take us too long!'

'Come on, Sparkles, let's get in the game,' said Flo, massaging her unicorn's shoulders. Jake was talking tactics with Pegasus and Darcy was helping her unicorn, Star,

get motivated with a loud song.

'Come *on*, Dave!' Mira whisper-shouted
into her unicorn's ear. She really wanted that
prize! Dave's eyes flickered open . . . and then
closed again. He shifted into another sleeping
position. Mira kept trying to shove him awake
but it was no use. He was going to snooze

through the carrot dig!

'Three ... two ... one ... GO!' said Miss
Glitterhorn.

The children watched expectantly as all
the unicorns except Dave trotted elegantly
into the pumpkin patch. Then they stopped
and looked at each other. A few of them

sniffed the ground. They wandered around the pumpkin patch for a while, looking a bit confused. Sparkles and Brave walked into each other. None of them dug up any carrots.

'Shall we go and help them?' said Freya.

'That might be an idea,' said Miss Glitterhorn. And so Class Red went over to help the unicorns with their search.

Mira decided to try rolling Dave into the pumpkin patch. Maybe his special ability to find his treasure would kick in if he was a bit nearer? Though that didn't seem to be helping the other unicorns. Princess had got her hoof caught in a bush and Firework was digging up some flowers.

'I found a treasure carrot!' yelled Seb. 'Oh no, wait, it's just some nuts.'

A cross-looking squirrel scurried over and snatched the nuts. It buried them again and then scurried away.

'Come on, Brave,' said Raheem to his UBFF. 'We can just triangulate the coordinates I logged last month.' Brave blinked at him.

'Did you find yours, Darcy? Well done!' said Mira as she saw her friend throwing a carrot up into the air.

'Nope. I brought this with me,' said Darcy. 'Star and I have decided ours is lost forever.'

'It is usually much quicker than this,' said Miss Glitterhorn. 'Perhaps no one wants the

chocolate-egg prize . . .'

Next to Mira, Dave's eyes snapped open. The mention of chocolate had done the trick! He leaped up from where Mira had just rolled him on to the edge of the pumpkin patch, knocking her backwards. Then he zoomed around the patch, his legs a blur, sending up showers of soil. Mira peered through the clouds of dirt, wondering if Dave had found his treasure. But she could see he was digging in lots of different places. What was he up to?

'Pegasus has found his treasure carrot!' called Jake smugly. 'We WIN!' He picked up the treasure from one of the freshly dug holes and waved it in the air.

'But Dave found it!' said Mira.

'Um, Jake?' said Raheem. 'I don't think that's a treasure carrot. I think it's a treasure . . . poo?'

They all peered more closely and saw that Raheem was right.

'ARGH!' yelled Jake, dropping the treasure poo.

'Princess found a treasure poo too!' said Freya. Next to her, Princess was looking down at another hole with a poo perched on it. Around the pumpkin patch were all the holes that Dave had dug, and they all contained poos.

'Is there a prize for finding treasure poos?' asked Seb, hopefully poking one with a stick.

Mira was dodging around all the treasure

poo-holes looking for her UBFF. Then she saw him. He was sitting right in front of Miss Glitterhorn – next to a big pile of carrots!

'Dave found all the carrots!' said Tamsin.

'And replaced them all with poos!' said Seb.

'Does that mean he wins the prize?' said Mira, hope rising in her chest. Dave never won ANYTHING.

'Um, yes, I suppose he does,' said Miss Glitterhorn, looking a bit surprised at the turn the treasure hunt had taken.

'YAY FOR DAVE!' yelled Mira and her classmates clapped.

Miss Glitterhorn put a little basket of chocolate eggs in front of Dave. 'And perhaps

as Dave has been kind enough to find all the carrots, he'd also like to share his prize,' the teacher said with a smile.

'YAAAAAY!' cheered Class Red. But Dave had already eaten the chocolate eggs.

CHAPTER TWO
Treasure-Egg Mystery

After Dave had also eaten all the treasure carrots, Class Red, their unicorns and Miss Glitterhorn all started walking back to school because there was no more treasure to find, just holes filled with poo. As they went, Raheem was explaining how all the poo would actually be good for fertilising next year's pumpkins, Jake was complaining about Dave hogging all the treasure and Dave was burping happily.

'Well done!' said Mira, giving her UBFF a

scratch behind the ears.

Dave burped again, and then started to splutter.

'What is it, Dave?' said Mira, feeling a bit alarmed.

Dave snorted and spat something on the floor. It looked like an egg. Mira stopped to pick it up, as the other children and unicorns walked on towards the school.

It wasn't a real egg. It was made of plastic and had soil on it. Mira guessed Dave must have gobbled it up when he'd dug up the carrots. It was very light, but when Mira shook it she could hear there was something inside.

'Hey guys, look at this . . .' she began. But then she realised that the rest of Class Red were out of sight. She quickly put the egg in her pocket and dragged Dave quickly back to school. She couldn't wait to show her friends the treasure egg!

Mira and Dave caught up with the rest of Class Red just as they got to the stables. Other Unicorn School classes were coming back from their own sunrise vegetable digs. Dave clambered on to the nearest bale of hay for a snooze.

'Guys, you won't believe what I found!' said Mira, running up to Darcy and Raheem.

But her friends and the rest of Class Red were listening to Mira's sister Rani, who was telling them all about something and casually eating a chocolate egg.

'I mean, winning the sunrise carrot dig is great,' Rani was saying, 'but that's just a warm-up. The Longest Day of the Year is basically the best day at Unicorn School. There's LOADS of treasure to find. Last year Angelica and I found pretty much all of it.'

Class Red ooohed in appreciation.

'Then we felt sorry for everyone else so we buried it all again,' said Rani, and had another chomp of her chocolate egg.

'Dave and I found some treasure!' said Mira,

stepping forward and waving the plastic egg.

Everyone turned to look at her.

Rani peered at the egg. 'What is that?' she

said.

'It's a TREASURE EGG,' said Mira,

holding it up to Rani's face.

'Ew, don't let it touch me!' said Rani, wrinkling her nose. 'Did you find it in a bin?'

'No!' said Mira indignantly. She wiped some of the soil off the egg. 'Dave dug it up.'

Rani gave her a pitying look. 'You can't dig up a pebble and call it treasure,' she said.

'It's not a pebble!' said Mira. The disappointment felt hot in her chest and she was starting to feel annoyed too. Everyone was meant to be excited about the treasure and Rani was ruining it! 'It's hollow. I think there's something inside ...'

She shook the egg. Class Red came a bit closer to try and listen.

'Probably just dirt inside. Or a tiny poo,' said Rani with a shrug.

Mira sighed. Sometimes she wished her sister wasn't at Unicorn School. She put the egg back in her pocket as her best friends, Darcy and Raheem, came over.

'Don't worry, Mira,' said Darcy. 'I liked your

bin pebble.'

'It's not a pebble!' said Mira.

'It's okay, Mira – pebbles are cool!' said Raheem. 'I'll make you one of my *Rocks Rock* badges if you like?'

'Thanks Raheem,' said Mira. 'But I really think this is a treasure egg with a secret message inside.' She shook the egg again. The sound was very faint, but she could definitely hear it.

'WOW!' said Darcy, and Raheem's eyes went wide.

Mira grinned back at her friends. Finally, they were getting excited about her treasure! 'See?' she said.

'Huh?' said Darcy. 'Oh sorry, I wasn't listening – I just heard Rani say that last year she and Angelica found an egg that shot rainbow lasers!'

'So awesome!' said Raheem and he and Darcy moved a bit closer to Rani to hear the rest of her story.

Mira sighed and turned the egg over in her hand. She could see a little line going around it, which must be where it opened. She tried to prize it open, but it wouldn't budge. Mira walked over to the hay bale where Dave was having his nap.

'We'll just solve the treasure-egg mystery on our own, Dave,' she said, giving him a scratch

behind the ears. Dave nuzzled her hand in his sleep. Mira felt a happy glow. At least she had her UBFF to solve the mystery with!

Then Dave did one of his superpowered stink farts and Mira still felt happy, but also a bit sick.

ʊʊʊ

'What are you going to do to with the extra time?' said Flo as Class Red and their unicorns made their way into the canteen for breakfast.

'What do you mean?' said Flo's twin sister Freya.

'It's the Longest Day of the Year,' said Flo, 'so that means we have more time. I'm going to discover a planet.'

'Like extra time in football?' asked Seb.

'But *magical* extra time,' said Tamsin.

'Well, actually the time is the same,' said Raheem. 'It's just daytime for longer.'

'Yeah, Raheem is right,' said Jake. 'The time is the same but everything takes longer – so

one minute is like five hours.'

'That wasn't what I said at all!' said Raheem.

'Also, the teachers don't make us go to bed until the sun goes down,' said Jake. 'We're going to be awake for AGES!'

'We're going to be awake for AGES!!' Mira whooped as Class Red ran into the canteen. The teachers were already there, sitting down with large mugs of coffee.

'What do you think we'll have for Longest Day Breakfast?' said Mira as they grabbed their breakfast trays.

'I don't know but you have to eat it really slowly,' said Flo.

It turned out that Longest Day Breakfast

was pancakes and maple syrup, which was Mira's favourite. Class Red cheered and Dave did a celebratory bum-wiggle dance until the PE teacher, Miss Hind, yelled at him to get down off the breakfast table.

As Mira was finishing her second pancake, and Dave was finishing his eleventh, the Unicorn School headteacher, Madame Shetland, stood up at the front of the canteen to tell them about the Longest Day of the Year activities.

'Good morning, everyone,' said Madame Shetland.

'Good morning, Madame Shetland,' chorused the Unicorn School pupils through

mouthfuls of pancake. Mira accidentally forgot to join in because she was thinking again about the treasure egg in her pocket. If the Longest Day meant they did have more time, then maybe she could solve the mystery AND do all the activities ...

'Welcome to the Longest Day of the Year,' said Madame Shetland. 'Many exciting and engaging challenges lie ahead of you and your unicorns. Keep prepared and stay alert, for there is treasure to find ... yes, Darcy?'

'Is the treasure chocolate eggs?' said Darcy, who was sitting next to Mira.

'Perhaps,' said Madame Shetland. 'But treasure doesn't have to be something you

can pick up. It could also be discovering an interesting fact, or learning a new skill.'

'But are there chocolate eggs as well?' said Darcy.

'Yes,' said Madame Shetland.

'YAAAAY,' cheered everyone.

'The MOST IMPORTANT thing,' said Madame Shetland, raising her voice to quieten down the cheering, 'is that you take your time. We want you to get as much out of this as possible.'

'And to stay out of our way all day,' said Miss Hind.

'Hahaha,' laughed Madame Shetland. 'Yes, very good, Miss Hind!'

Miss Hind stared stonily ahead and folded her arms.

'And finally,' said Madame Shetland, 'there will be a special prize for bringing back the most unusual or interesting piece of treasure.'

Mira sat up straighter in her seat. If she could solve the treasure-egg mystery, then surely she would win? Then everyone would be listening to *her* treasure hunting stories . . .

As Madame Shetland continued to talk, Mira caught Rani's eye. Rani mouthed, 'Loser.' Mira narrowed her eyes and stuck out her tongue.

'Are you okay, dear?' said Miss Ponytail, the Art teacher, peering at Mira with concern. 'Is it wind?'

'Oh! No, I was just ... stretching my
tongue,' said Mira. 'I want to be really ready
for the treasure hunt.'

'Oh yes, good to be fully prepared,' said Miss
Ponytail, as Jake gave Mira a strange look and
Rani got told off for laughing so much.

'... and when the activities are complete,'
Madame Shetland was saying, 'there will be
the final tradition – the Longest Day Surprise!'

'Yes, don't be late for the party,' said Miss Hind.

'Or whatever the surprise may be!' said Madame Shetland, waggling her hands mysteriously.

'Last year it was a party!' said Jimmy from Class Blue.

'And the year before,' chimed in Yusuf from Class Indigo.

'Well,' said Madame Shetland. 'You never know.'

Soon it was time for Longest Day Breakfast to finish and the activities to begin, but Class Red had to wait because Tamsin had taken half an hour to chew one mouthful of toast.

CHAPTER THREE
Poo Pick-up and Pool Party

The activities were divided into three different activity stations and the classes were doing them in different orders, so it didn't get too crowded.

'Can I be team leader?' said Jake. Jake *always* wanted to be team leader.

'We won't be having team leaders today, as we want you to all work together,' said Miss Glitterhorn. 'But who's going to carry Class Red's treasure basket?'

'Ooh, I will!' said Darcy, waving her arms in the air.

'Brilliant – thank you, Darcy!' said Miss Glitterhorn.

'That's not fair!' said Jake and Pegasus snorted indignantly.

Darcy came to the front and took the basket from Miss Glitterhorn.

'As long as you don't eat all the chocolate eggs yourself,' grumbled Jake.

'I can't promise that, sorry,' said Darcy.

'And in the basket you'll find your map,' said Miss Glitterhorn. 'You must take special care of it as you'll need it to navigate your way around. So –'

'Oh, no thank you,' said Darcy, handing the map back.

'I'll take care of the map!' said Raheem. 'I brought a compass in my emergency bumbag.'

'I wanted the map!' said Jake.

'And we've got one special job left,' said

Miss Glitterhorn. 'Who's going to be in charge of . . .'

'Me, ME! I'll do it!' said Jake, jumping up and down.

'. . . collecting the poo,' finished Miss Glitterhorn. 'Oh, that's wonderful – thank you, Jake. It's going to be a long day out for the unicorns and it's so important to clean up after them. Plus, you can bring the poo back to fertilise the pumpkin patch!'

Jake stared as Miss Glitterhorn wheeled out a small, green cart with a scoop hanging from the side. On the side of the cart was faded writing saying THE POO CART with a drawing of poo next to a face with crossed out eyes.

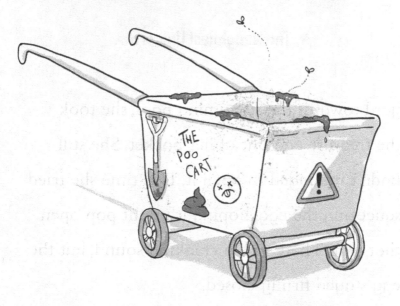

'It was decorated by Unicorn School students,' explained Miss Glitterhorn.

Raheem checked the map. A little trail led to the first activity station: the Unicorn School swimming pool.

'Off you go, Class Red,' said Miss Glitterhorn. 'Good luck and I'll see you later for the party, I mean surprise!'

As Mira trotted on Dave across the stable

yard towards the swimming pool, she took the treasure egg out of her pocket. She still hadn't managed to open it. This time she tried squeezing the egg, hoping it might pop open that way. There was a creaking sound, but the egg stayed firmly closed.

'What are you doing?' came a voice that startled Mira, nearly making her drop the egg.

Jake was riding next to her on Pegasus, who was pulling the poo cart. Usually he and Pegasus didn't ride near Mira and Dave because Jake said Pegasus was allergic to Dave's super stinkfarts.

'Nothing,' said Mira. She knew Jake would think her treasure-egg mystery was silly.

'What are you doing?'

'Your unicorn has pooed already,' said Jake. 'I need to collect it.'

Mira turned around. Sure enough, Dave had done a giant poo right in the middle of the path. Jake held out the scoop, but Mira waved it away. 'It's okay, I have my own,' she said. Mira always carried a poo shovel, because Dave did about five times as many poos as other unicorns.

As Mira shovelled up the poo, Jake held out a bin bag. 'Check there isn't any treasure in it first,' he said.

'Um, I think it's just poo,' said Mira.

'You've got to stay alert for treasure at all

times,' Jake said. 'That's what my dad says – and he was the treasure-hunt champion every year when he was at Unicorn School. We have all the trophies in our house.'

'Wow,' said Mira. Her parents didn't have any Unicorn School trophies. Her dad just had a T-shirt from the time he won a hot-dog eating contest (she had been proud of him, though). Rani had plenty of Unicorn School medals, but that was no help because if she ever tried asking her sister for advice, Rani just growled at her until she got out of her room.

'What other tips does your dad have?' Mira asked.

'He says that with treasure hunting you have to think inside the box,' said Jake.

'Do you mean think *outside* the box?' said Mira.

'No,' said Jake. 'That's what everyone does. So you need to do the opposite. Anyway, we have to go. Princess has pooed by the swimming-pool entrance.'

Jake and Pegasus trotted away, pulling the poo cart behind them. Mira looked down at her egg. She wasn't sure that Jake's tips had helped her, but she was determined to think like a treasure hunter and solve the treasure-egg mystery!

ᴗᴗᴗ

PHWEEEEEEEEEEEEEP!

Miss Hind blew her whistle loudly as they all lined up by the swimming pool. Class Yellow and their unicorns were there too, and Miss Hind was handing out life jackets. 'Attention, Class Red and Class Yellow!' she said. 'Get ready for your first activity.'

Mira looked at the pool. There were two lines of four floats tied together with rope stretching out across the water. On the fifth float, sitting on a cushion, was a large, glittery purple box.

'On your unicorns, you must run along the floats without falling in,' said Miss Hind.

'That's EASY,' said Jake, but everyone else looked at each other and Mira gulped. It didn't look easy to her!

'The team who gets to the end will open the special glittery box and see what's inside.'

'Oooooh,' said Class Red and Class Yellow.

'It's VERY hard,' Miss Hind continued. 'Many of our most talented unicorns have tried over the years and hardly anyone has done it.'

Mira looked at her UBFF, who was currently licking his bum like a cat. Dave didn't usually enjoy sports and one of his biggest talents was hiding to get out of PE. But sometimes he surprised everyone.

Would this be one of those times?

'BUT to help encourage you I have a treat for the winning team,' continued Miss Hind. She held up a basket of chocolate eggs.

Dave immediately made a lunge towards Miss Hind, but Mira was too quick for him. She wrestled her unicorn and put him in a bumlock, which is like a headlock but for the bum. Dave was wriggling and trying to get free.

'Okay, team,' said Jake, calling Class Red into a huddle. 'We are out to win this. Watch closely, we'll show you how it's done.'

He hopped up on to his unicorn's back. Pegasus stepped tentatively on to the first float, slipped to the side and fell in.

'Oh, that does look easy,' said Flo, riding forward on Sparkles. They stepped on to the first float and dived off to the side.

'GO FLO!' yelled Flo, as she bobbed around in the water.

'Come on, Class Red, get in the game!' called Darcy from the poolside, where she and Star were lying on deckchairs.

'We need some new tactics,' said Jake, who

was out of the pool now and dripping wet. He squeezed the water out of Pegasus's mane.

'What about running and leaping?' said Mira, as Dave continued to try and wriggle free of her bumlock. 'Maybe then you could jump over the first few floats and not have as many to run across?'

'Good plan!' said Freya. 'Okay, Princess, let's g—'

But Princess had already shot forward. She galloped up to the edge of the pool and jumped. Mira and the rest of Class Red stared open-mouthed as Freya and Princess sailed through the air. They'd jumped further than the first two floats!

Unfortunately, they'd taken off right down the middle of the two lines of floats, and they landed in the water.

On the Class Yellow side, a girl called Abiola got to float three. They'd almost made it to the glittery box!

Now it was Seb and Firework. They decided just to go as fast as they could . . . and they got to float two! But still no glittery box.

Tamsin and Moondance went next.

They decided to jump from float to float, and were very wobbly, but they got to float three!

Next up were Raheem and Brave. Raheem was looking nervous, while Brave was pawing the ground with his hoof, eager to get going.

'You'll be brilliant!' Mira said encouragingly.

Raheem didn't reply, but he nodded, his eyes squeezed tightly shut. Brave trotted forward. They hopped from the poolside on to the first float. Then the second.

And then the third . . .

'Go Raheem and Brave!' cheered Class Red. Mira jumped up and down.

As they stepped on to the fourth float, Raheem opened his eyes. He looked around in surprise. 'WE'RE NEARLY THERE!' he yelled, startling Brave, who lost his footing and sent them both splashing into the water.

'That was the best so far!' Mira grinned at her best friend as Raheem climbed out of the pool.

Raheem grinned back. 'Thanks!' he said and wrapped Brave up in a towel.

It was Mira and Dave's turn now.

'Right, Dave,' Mira said. 'We'll WIN

Miss Hind's chocolate eggs – then they'll taste even better!'

Dave snorted grumpily.

'I'll let you out of the bumlock,' said Mira, 'but you can't run off, okay? Otherwise we won't have the chance to win!'

Dave snorted again, but he stopped wriggling. Mira let go of Dave's bum and quickly hopped round and on to his back. The little unicorn began walking obediently towards the side of the pool. Mira felt a little glow of pride. See? Dave wasn't *always* misbehaving!

'Come on!' called Miss Hind, as another pair from Class Yellow splashed into the pool.

'If no one completes the activity, soon I'll have to start eating these chocolate eggs myself.'

Dave bucked Mira off on to the grass and made a dash towards Miss Hind. This time Mira wasn't quick enough – she dived forward to tackle him but missed.

'NO, DAVE!' yelled Mira, racing after him.

The rest of Class Red tried to stop Dave, but he dodged and wove his way around them.

Miss Hind's eyes went wide as the unicorn charged towards her. He made a leap and caught the basket handle in his mouth, pulling it away from her. But Miss Hind's grip was

strong. She yanked the basket back, taking
Dave with it. His little legs flailed in the air
as she tried to shake him off.

'Do a
bumlock!' yelled
Mira. 'Do a
bumlock!'
But Miss Hind
either didn't hear or didn't
know what a bumlock was. So
Mira dashed forward and managed to wrap
her arms around Dave's bum. Miss Hind gave

the basket an extra hard yank and pulled it free from Dave.

The force of the yank also sent the basket spinning out of Miss Hind's hand. The basket flipped round, and all the chocolate eggs went flying up into the air and down, down down . . .

Into

the

swimming

pool.

CHAPTER FOUR
Magic Blankets and Messages

Dave immediately started galloping towards the swimming pool after the eggs, with Mira still clinging on. Mira braced herself for hitting the water. There was a **THUMP** and a *SPLASH* ... but then they were going upwards again! Dave had bounced off the first float on his bum and caught a chocolate egg in mid-air!

Mira could hear cheers as Dave caught another chocolate egg. With another thump

and a splash Dave's bum hit the second
float. **BOUNCE!** Dave caught a THIRD
chocolate egg and they bum-bounced the
third float and then the fourth. Dave caught
the last two eggs at once and did a loud,
happy burp.

Incredibly, they were heading towards the
final float, on which sat the purple glittery
box. Mira braced herself for another bum-
bounce . . . but this time they landed flat on
the float with the biggest thump and splash
yet – and stayed there.

On the poolside, Class Red went wild.
Even Class Yellow were clapping.

Mira sat up, feeling a bit dazed.

But gradually it dawned on her – they had run across all the floats!

'Well done, Dave!' she said as her little unicorn climbed to his feet and shook the water off himself like a dog. She picked up the purple glittery box.

'Well, I suppose that means you win,' said Miss Hind from the poolside, folding her arms. She was still looking quite cross about the chocolate-egg wrestle.

'Open the egg! Open the box!' called Seb and Tamsin.

Mira carefully opened the purple glittery box. Inside was a small, green blanket.

That was strange treasure, Mira thought. She was about to hold it up to show the others when she saw something else. Where Dave had stood up, directly under his bum, Mira saw her special treasure egg. And it had finally popped open! Dave must have landed on it bum first. And just poking out of it was

a folded-up piece of paper . . .

∪∪∪

'Maybe it's a magic blanket?' said Tamsin.

Now everyone had dried off and they were peering at the small green blanket in their treasure basket.

'What would a magic blanket do?' said Freya.

'Fly?' suggested Tamsin.

'It's a bit small,' said Darcy.

'Perhaps it's just for flying hamsters?' said Seb.

Raheem frowned. 'Maybe it isn't a blanket at all. Maybe it's a napkin. Or a tiny flag?'

'Or alien knickers,' said Flo thoughtfully.

'Well, it's still treasure,' said Jake. 'And it's all we've got since SOMEONE ate all our chocolate eggs.' He narrowed his eyes at Dave.

'We wouldn't have any treasure at all if Dave hadn't done his bum-bouncing!' said Mira. 'Anyway – that's not ALL we've got . . .' She pulled the soggy secret message out of her pocket.

'Ugh, what's that?' said a voice from behind her.

It was Rani. Class Orange and Class Green were arriving at the swimming pool, and Rani was at the front, carrying the Class Orange basket.

'It's a secret mess—' Mira started to say.

'I FOUND A GLOW-IN-THE-DARK
EGG IN THE FEARSOME FOREST!'
interrupted Rani.

'Wow!' said Tamsin and Seb at the same
time. Class Red all
crowded round Rani's
basket.

'That's cool you
found a secret mess,
though, Mira!' said
Flo, turning back
briefly as Rani was
showing them all the
treasure she'd found.

Mira sighed. But then she thought to herself
how impressed everyone would be when she
and Dave solved the treasure-egg mystery
by themselves and surprised them all! Mira
unfolded the message. The loopy writing was
quite faded, and some of the ink had gone
blurry from falling in the swimming pool, but
luckily she could still make out the words.

Sheltered and hidden with sparkles galore,
I'm number two, not one, three or four
Green all around and inside the box,
Is the one special treasure – X marks the spot!

It was a riddle – and surely it must lead to
the special treasure! She had been right all
along! The only problem was that Mira had
no idea what the riddle meant.

'What do you think, Dave?' she said,
holding the piece of paper out to him.

Dave sniffed it thoughtfully. Then he
tried to eat it. Mira quickly reached for her
emergency snack bag and gave him a Jammy
Dodger. She read through the riddle a few
more times.

'Stop DAWDLING, Mira and Dave!' called
Miss Hind. 'You need to get to the next
activity station.'

Mira looked up to see that all of Class Red

and Class Yellow were ready to go. She put the riddle back in her pocket and hopped on Dave's back. They went quickly over to join their classmates.

'You were a worthy opponent, Dave,' said Miss Hind as they passed. 'Let me know if you would consider a future in Unicorn Wrestling.'

Dave blinked and gave a surprised burp.

'So the map says we go to the Crystal Maze Mine next!' said Raheem.

ᑌᑌᑌ

Class Red and Class Yellow trotted out of the school grounds and towards the Crystal Maze Mine, at the base of the Crystal Mountains.

'I can't wait to see all the rocks in the Mine!' said Raheem.

'I'm going to make a glitter ball from slime,' said Darcy. 'It'll be even bigger than that one I made for the school disco. And ten times as sparkly.'

Mira was about to tell Darcy that sounded awesome, but then she had a thought. Hadn't the riddle mentioned something about sparkles?

She got it out to check.

Sheltered and hidden with sparkles galore . . .

Maybe the treasure was in the Mine?

The crystals were sparkly. The riddle had said the place was *green all around*. Was there a green part of the Mine? And then there was the line about numbers. *I'm number two, not one, three or four.* What did that mean?

'Poo alert!' said Jake, riding up next to them. 'Make way for the cart!' Then he looked at the piece of paper in Mira's hand. 'What's that?'

'Oh, nothing,' said Mira, folding it up and reaching for her poo shovel. Dave's poo was so giant it was blocking the path, but luckily they were at the back of the group. 'Definitely not TOP-SECRET TREASURE or anything like that . . .'

Jake laughed. 'Well, obviously! Like you and

Dave would be able to find top-secret treasure. You're not highly trained like me and Pegasus.'

Mira felt a little bubble of anger rise up as she shovelled the poo into a bag. But she swallowed it down. When she and Dave were Treasure-Hunt Champions, then everyone would see!

'We've been practising the treasure hunting walk for like, six hours a day,' Jake continued. 'It's the walk all treasure hunters do. My dad showed me.'

'Does your dad say anything about riddles?' asked Mira, wondering if there might be any treasure hunting tips that would help her solve it.

'Yeah!' said Jake. 'He said solving clues is
the hardest part of treasure hunting. I mean,
if you gave me a riddle I'd probably solve it in
five seconds or something, but that's because
the treasure hunting part of my brain is so
big.'

'Did he tell you *how* you solve riddles?' said
Mira.

Jake thought. 'He says you have to take one
clue at a time. And that the answer is usually
under your nose. Anyway – come on! Put
the bag in the poo cart. I don't want to be
late for when I get crowned Treasure-Hunt
Champion!'

'Yeah . . .' said Mira, tying up the bag.

She imagined putting on the Treasure-Hunt Champion crown. Was there a crown? There *should* be a crown. And maybe some kind of golden sword? And Rani would have to put the crown on her head – and probably bow and kneel to her a few times. She pictured the rest of Class Red applauding and shouting, 'Mira's the best!' and, 'All hail Queen Mira!' and, 'We should have known it was a treasure egg and not a bin pebble!'

'Er . . . Mira?' said Jake. 'Hello? You haven't spoken for three minutes and you're doing that wave that the Queen does.'

Mira blinked and came out of her daydream. 'I was just . . . thinking about

waving at all the sparkly rocks in the Crystal Maze Mine.' She popped the bag in the poo cart.

'Okay . . .' said Jake. He hopped back on to his unicorn. 'Ride on, Pegasus!'

Then Dave coughed politely. He'd done another giant poo.

CHAPTER FIVE
Into the Mine!

'You are HERE! We thought you had PERISHED!' said Ms Dazzleflank the Drama teacher as Mira, Jake, Dave and Pegasus emerged from the woods. She swooned dramatically on to a pile of leaves. Her unicorn, Shakespeare, fanned her with his hoof.

'Are you okay, Ms Dazzleflank?' said Freya.

'Has SHE perished?' said Tamsin.

'Now they're here can we go in and make a GLITTERBALL?' said Darcy.

'Did you guys get lost?' asked Raheem.

'Dave did two giant poos and it took AGES to scoop them up,' said Jake.

'I said it would be poo-related!' said Seb.

'I said you'd probably been eaten by bats,' said Flo.

'Glitterball?' said Darcy.

'Right, Classes Red and Yellow!' said Ms Dazzleflank. She'd got up from her swoon and was looking at her watch. 'The ancient treasure hunting ways are unfettered by the sands of time ... However, you are starting late so you will need to be quick.' The teacher took in a deep breath. 'I will now mime the activity.'

They all watched as Ms Dazzleflank first whirled her arms in circles, then did large skips around the clearing, and then flung her hands in random directions, like she was swatting invisible flies. She froze for a moment or two, and then she took a bow.

Classes Red and Yellow looked at her blankly.

'Fine,' said the drama teacher. 'You go in two separate entrances. You have to take a train ride through the caves and then when you get to the central cave there will be a Glitter Grab.'

'Ooooh!' said Classes Red and Yellow.

Mira didn't know what a Glitter Grab was, but it sounded exciting!

'I remember that from last year!' said Abiola from Class Yellow. 'There's glitter flying around everywhere and you have to grab tokens.'

'Yes,' said Ms Dazzleflank. 'And the team that grabs the gold token will get this.'

She held up another purple glittery box. 'Now, are you all ready?'

'Come on, guys,' said Darcy. 'If I'm going to make fifty glitterballs, we need to get in there now!'

All the children in Classes Red and Yellow were hopping up and down, eager to get going. Mira thought the Glitter Grab sounded super fun. She would have to make sure she solved the riddle and found the treasure really quickly, so they didn't miss any of it.

Ms Dazzleflank showed Class Red to a little steam train with wagons attached. Mira remembered going on it before, the last time they'd come to the Crystal Maze Mine.

Then the teacher took Class Yellow to show them their entrance, which was further round the mountainside. Class Red all immediately started arguing about who would sit at the front.

'It doesn't matter,' said Mira. 'We just need to get going. The sooner we're in there, the sooner we'll be at the Glitter Grab!' And the sooner we'll solve the riddle . . . she thought to herself with a little thrill of excitement.

∪∪∪

The train track dipped as they went down the entrance tunnel. Glitter and sparkles from the walls of the cave whooshed past on either side of Mira. It was like being on a rollercoaster!

She tried to
look out for any flashes of
green, like the riddle said, but they
were going so fast that all the colours
were blurring. Mira had been thinking
about what Jake said about taking one clue
at a time. Maybe if she found the sparkles
first, then she'd find the green? The numbers
clue was harder, but maybe when she found
the green that would become clear too?

They whizzed through one dark sparkly

cave and into another. This one had a big lake which reflected the sparkles even more. 'Ooooooh,' called everyone and Darcy took a picture on her phone. The caves could definitely be the sparkles from the riddle, but Mira couldn't see any green.

They trundled on into the next cave, which was huge and had lots of tunnels going off it.

'Stop!' called Darcy. 'I recognise this place from last time I made glitterballs! I want to find more glitter!'

'We can't stop,' Freya called back. She was in the driving cabin at the front. 'We have to get to the Glitter Grab!'

'It might be fun to explore those tunnels, though,' said Seb. 'Maybe we can find some treasure for the basket.'

'I was about to say that!' said Jake from behind Mira. He and Pegasus had had to go

82

in the last wagon because it was the only one that would fit the poo cart in it.

'Okay,' said Freya. She pressed the brake. The train creaked to a stop and Class Red and their unicorns climbed out. Mira clenched her fists excitedly. This would give her the perfect opportunity to find her treasure!

'We have to be quick,' Freya reminded them.

'Don't worry, I'll only make thirty glitterballs this time,' said Darcy, as she trotted off on Star to find the Glitter Slime Gorge.

'And I'll only collect thirty special rocks!' said Raheem, unfurling a large *Rocks Rock* bag.

Mira nudged Dave out of the wagon. 'Come on, Dave!' she said. 'Let's solve our riddle!'

Dave didn't move. He looked back at the train track leading out of the big cave.

Mira knew he was worried about missing the Glitter Grab. 'It's okay, Dave – we'll be back in time,' she promised. 'We'll win ALL the chocolate AND when I'm Queen Mira I can give you all the chocolate you want forever.'

Dave tilted his head to the side and looked a bit confused. But then he snorted again and started walking next to Mira, turning his head back to the train a few times.

There were lots of tunnels leading off the huge cave. Everyone was picking different ones to explore. Mira had a thought.

I'm number two, not one, three or four . . .

What if that meant to check in the *second* tunnel?

They followed Jake and Pegasus, who were about to head down the tunnel to the second cave. Mira saw that they were strutting and waggling their elbows, which she thought must be the treasure hunting walk. The poo cart bumped and rattled behind them on the rocky ground.

'Why don't you leave it by the train?' said Mira.

'Er, because some of us take our responsibilities seriously, Mira,' Jake replied. 'What kind of poo collector would I be if left the poo cart behind? Anyway, poo can strike

at any time.' Pegasus gave Dave a wary look.

The second cave was sparkly, but it wasn't green. Mira and Dave left Jake and Pegasus in there turning over stones, because apparently Jake's dad said a treasure hunter 'leaves no stone unturned'. They came back into the big cave of tunnels and Mira decided to try the

next tunnel. Maybe the numbers clue meant
something else — like there would be four
caves in one of the tunnels? Or four hiding
places in one of the caves? It was all starting
to hurt Mira's head a bit so she decided just
to search as many caves as possible. But every
cave she went into didn't quite fit — either it

was green but not sparkly, or sparkly but not green. One of the caves had four holes in the wall, each the perfect size for a treasure chest, but it was purple and there were no sparkles at all. The next cave they went into was pitch black and they found Flo and Sparkles in there trying to summon a ghost. Mira was feeling more and more disappointed, and Dave was getting grumpier and grumpier because of all the running around.

They came back into the huge cave as Freya was getting everyone back on to the train.

'We need to get into the main cave for the Glitter Grab,' Freya said. 'Is everyone here? Where's Darcy?'

'Here I am!' Darcy came strutting out on Star. They all gasped. Darcy had her arms full of glitterballs – but that wasn't the surprising thing. Darcy LOVED glitter. The surprising thing was the way Darcy and Star were covered from head to toe in glittery slime and glinting, green gems. They shone in the gloom like a pair of traffic lights.

Mira froze. *Sparkles galore* AND *green all around* . . .

'You look amazing!' said Tamsin.

'We decided to decorate the glitterballs with emeralds from the Emerald Cave,' said Darcy. 'And then we decided to decorate ourselves.'

Emerald cave? thought Mira. 'BE RIGHT BACK!' she shouted.

CHAPTER SIX
Emerald Explorations

Dave snorted crossly as they sprinted down the tunnel that Darcy had just come from. Then, as they reached the Glitter Slime Gorge (which led to the Emerald Cave), he sat down and refused to move.

After trying to drag him along Mira gave up. 'Okay. You stay here and I'll just run in and grab the treasure and run straight back!' said Mira excitedly.

She ran into the Emerald Cave. On all sides

the sparkly green gems dazzled her. It was *definitely* green all around AND there were sparkles ... But as Mira's eyes adjusted to the brightness, she could see that apart from the gems in the walls, there wasn't anything else in the cave. She ran quickly around all the edges to check if there was anything she could count, or any gaps or places where a box could be hidden. But there weren't – and there was no sign of an X.

Mira sighed as she came back through the Glitter Slime Gorge and collected Dave.

'I guess I was wrong,' she said. 'Sorry, Dave!'

Dave sniffed sympathetically and rubbed his head on Mira's hand. He never stayed cross

with her for very long. Also, the detour had given him time to eat A LOT of glitter slime.

They sprinted back into the main cave and jumped back aboard the train.

'I think it's only a couple of caves away,' said Freya, as she pressed the 'GO' button. 'It sounds like Class Yellow are already there!'

Mira could hear shouts nearby. She hoped Class Yellow hadn't already grabbed all the tokens! 'Sorry I made us late!' she said as the train trundled into the next cave, which had a waterfall in it.

'I said we should have left you behind,' called Jake from the last wagon. 'But Freya said that's not what teammates do.'

'I thought you'd been eaten by bats again,' said Flo.

Suddenly Class Red were surrounded by glitter. Not just on the walls, but flying in the air on every side. There, in the middle of the cave, were Class Yellow, leaping up and down among the glitter and snatching at the air. The Glitter Grab!

'Quick!' yelled Freya.

They climbed down from the train and all hurried towards the Glitter Grab. Jake and Pegasus were hurrying and doing the treasure hunting walk at the same time, which didn't look easy.

'ARRGGGGGGH!' Flo came charging past them all, her arms whirling around in circles.

Mira saw a boy from Class Yellow grab a silver token.

'THERE'S THE GOLDEN TOKEN!' yelled Seb.

Seb and Firework got there – just as Flo and Sparkles leaped up and grabbed the golden token out of the air.

υυυ

Class Red trundled back through the caves on their train. It was a bit weighed down by Darcy's glitterballs and Raheem's rocks, plus they were going uphill now, so the train was going very slowly.

By the time they got out of the Mine,

Class Yellow had already gone ahead. But
Ms Dazzleflank was waiting to give them
their purple glittery box prize. She also
handed over some chocolate eggs, which went
into Class Red's treasure basket on Darcy's
lap. Mira quickly put Dave in a bumlock
again in case he tried to steal them.

Flo popped open the purple glittery box.
Inside was a brown paper bag full of seeds.

'AWESOME!' said Flo.

'Please may we exchange it for something
better?' said Darcy, peering over Flo's shoulder.

'Now, Class Red,' said Ms Dazzleflank
in a dramatic whisper. 'Be fleet of foot, for
adventures new awaken yonder!'

Class Red looked at each other again.

'I think that means we have to go to the next activity station,' said Freya.

'Yes, that's right,' said Ms Dazzleflank. And she waved them away, while Shakespeare struck more poses.

ᴗᴗᴗ

The next activity station was the Fearsome Forest. On the way Class Red decided to share out the chocolate eggs, because it was already feeling like a long time since breakfast and they had one more activity to do before they could eat at the party. Also they all knew that if they didn't eat them, then Dave would.

Although the tiny blanket and the bag
of seeds weren't as exciting as they'd
expected, they had added some of their own
collected treasures to the basket. There were
Darcy's glitterballs, Raheem's rocks and a
multicoloured leaf that Seb had
found by the swimming
pool. Flo said that
Gregory, the ghost
she'd summoned in
the Mine, was sitting
in the basket as well.
Tamsin and Freya were
still looking and Jake was going to put his
treasure in right at the end because his dad

said you always save the best treasure for last.

Mira couldn't wait to add her treasure to the basket. But she still needed to solve that riddle and FIND the treasure!

Dave let out tiny farts with every step as they trotted along the path. Mira knew this was a sign he was in a good mood. Ahead of

them the trees of the Fearsome Forest rose up,
their green leaves rustling in the warm breeze.
Dave's tiny farts kept tooting out, a bit like a
little trumpet. Mira started to laugh.

'You're right, Dave,' she said. 'We should stay
positive. We have loads of time to solve the
riddle. It's the Longest Day of the Year!'

'*Toot toot toot!*' replied Dave's trumpety bum.

'You know what, though?' Mira said, a new feeling of excitement tingling in her tummy. 'I have a feeling we're going to solve it really soon. Just in time for lunch!'

TOOT TOOT! Dave let out a not-so-tiny and very excited fart at the mention of lunch. Above their heads the leaves shook again. Mira stared up. Green leaves! And then she looked down. Green grass! The forest was *green all around*! But did it have *sparkles galore*? And what about the numbers?

One clue at a time, Mira reminded herself. One clue at a time!

CHAPTER SEVEN
Into the Fearsome Forest

When Class Red arrived at the clearing near the entrance to the Fearsome Forest, the teacher in charge had already left.

Dear Class Red,

(Unless you are all dead. In which case, sorry about that.)

You took so long to get here I had to give up waiting for you. See you at the ~~party~~ I mean, the surprise. I've left the instructions under the twigs.

Love (and sorry if you got eaten by a Fearsome

Forest Monster),

Mr Trotsky and Horatio

X

Freya ran over and picked up the instructions. '*So, the last activity is where your unicorns' skills in sniffing out treasure really come into play,*' she read out loud. '*Follow the forest trail to find the Longest Day Surprise!*'

Class Red chatted excitedly. Soon they would be at the surprise party!

'Where does the trail start?' asked Seb.

They all looked around the clearing.

As well as the main forest path, there were lots

of other openings in the trees, each with a different coloured flag.

'Ours must be the red one!' said Tamsin, pointing to an opening on the left.

'How do we follow the trail?' asked Raheem, sounding panicked. 'THIS ISN'T ON THE MAP!'

Freya looked back at the instructions. *'Your unicorns will sniff out the carrots, buried at different points along the trail, to guide you through.'*

'Like in the pumpkin patch!' said Tamsin.

Dave's nostrils twitched. Mira knew he was going to enjoy this activity!

'But make sure you stick together in the Fearsome Forest,' continued Freya. *'Don't leave the path!'*

Mira really wanted to help her team with the activity this time. But she also *really* wanted to solve her riddle. Perhaps, if she just happened to see some sparkles, or numbers, or a big X, while they were on the trail, then she could still find the special treasure without letting her team down? After all, she still needed something to put in the treasure basket. It was looking even fuller now, as Freya had added a snail shell that glowed like a pearl and Tamsin had found a green and yellow feather in a hedge.

Everyone stepped through the gap in the trees marked by the red flag.

'GET SNIFFING!' yelled Freya.

The unicorns all began sniffing the ground,
searching for the first carrot. Dave was more
animated than Mira had ever seen him,
snorting around tree roots and nudging
clumps of grass.

Meanwhile, Mira searched for sparkles. The sunlight glinting through the leaves was a bit sparkly if you squinted, but she didn't think it counted as *sparkles galore*. Some slimy snail trails on a tree root sort of glittered, but they were much more like snot than sparkles. Mira got the riddle out, to see if reading it again would help.

There was a sudden loud whinny.

'Dave found the first carrot!' called Raheem.

Sure enough, over by a little patch of weeds, her UBFF was digging up a carrot with a red tag on it. He gobbled down the carrot (and the tag) and then did a poo to replace the carrot, just like he had done in the sunrise carrot dig.

'Well done, Dave!' said Mira, giving his mane a stroke. Jake wrinkled his nose as he added the poo to the cart.

'So, it's this way!' said Freya, leading the way down a narrow path beside the weed patch. The rest of Class Red and their unicorns ran after her.

Sparkles tripped over something, which turned out to be the next carrot. She copied Dave and did a poo in his place, but her poo was neat and glittery. Everyone changed direction again. Then Dave found two more carrots and they were dashing down another forest path.

'I think we're doing the trail really quickly!'

said Raheem, riding up next to Mira. 'Thanks
to Dave.'

Mira grinned. Then she saw that he was
knitting something. 'What are you making?'
she said.

'Oh, it's a protection cloak,' said Raheem.
'To keep the sparkle spiders away.'

Brave gave a shiver. He was VERY scared
of sparkle spiders and the Fearsome Forest
was absolutely full of them.

Then Mira realised something. 'SPARKLE
SPIDERS!' she said.

'What?' said Raheem.

'Oh, um . . . nothing!' said Mira. 'Dave and I
are going to sniff out the next carrot over here!'

She dragged Dave to the edge of the path, where sparkle spiders usually hung around. Sure enough there was a little line of them, scuttling through the undergrowth.

Sheltered and hidden with sparkles galore . . .

Mira had a feeling that if she followed them back to the sparkle-spider nest, she'd find the treasure!

A bit further off the other unicorns were still sniffing for carrots. Dave kept straining to go and join them.

'We'll get back to the carrot trail really soon, Dave,' said Mira. 'Right now we're going to solve the mystery once and for all!'

UՍU

Mira had never seen so many sparkle spiders in one place! Their delicate shimmery webs hung in the trees all around her.

'It's like a spider city!' said Mira.

Dave shivered and snorted, sending sparkle spiders scurrying off in different directions. Mira knew her UBFF was still cross about being taken away from the carrot-sniffing and she did feel a bit guilty. It wasn't often that Unicorn School activities included Dave's Top Two Favourite Things – eating and pooing.

As she looked around, Mira realised that there were four nests. Perhaps there was something special about nest number two,

just like the riddle said!

Mira crept closer to the second nest, taking care not to dislodge any of the sparkly webs. She tried to ignore the spiders scuttling past her. Sparkle spiders were harmless, but she could see why the scuttling freaked people out. Behind her, Dave farted nervously.

The nest led to the bottom of a tree trunk.

And lying at the bottom of the tree trunk was a yellow metal box.

Green all around and inside the box . . .

'The riddle!' exclaimed Mira, startling a group of sparkle spiders.

She grabbed the box. A few sparkle spiders fell off it. Then she hopped back through

the nest and out on to the path with Dave
scurrying after her.

As soon as she was out of the nest, Mira
looked down at the box. Dave was already
sniffing it. Right by his nose, on the top left
corner, were written the letters 'XT'.

Mira gasped. First a box, and now *X marks
the spot!* She'd solved the riddle and found
the treasure!

There was the sound of breaking twigs behind them. Mira's heart leaped in her chest. Maybe the spiders were coming to get their treasure back?

'There you are!' said Raheem. Class Red and their unicorns were making their way through the trees towards Mira and Dave. 'But . . . why are you BY THE SPARKLE SPIDER NEST?'

Brave leaped behind Raheem with a screech, his hooves over his eyes.

'Finding treasure!' said Mira.

'Did you find the last purple glittery box?' said Freya.

'Is it twigs or something?' said Darcy.

'No, it's much better than that. It's my treasure-egg mystery!' Mira held the box above her head and danced around.

'What's a treasure-egg mystery?' asked Tamsin.

So Mira explained to them the whole story of the treasure-egg mystery. Even Jake looked impressed, though he didn't say anything.

'Let's open up the box!' said Freya and the rest of them cheered.

CHAPTER EIGHT
TREASURE!

Mira took a calming breath. This was it.
This was her moment!

'Behold ... the special treasure!' she said
as she opened the box.

Class Red gathered round her excitedly,
craning their necks to see. Inside the box
was ... a half-eaten cheese sandwich and
a banana.

'Huh?' said Mira.

Class Red looked a bit less excited.
Flo started clapping but then she stopped.

Only Dave looked pleased.

'Ooh, you've found my lunch!' said a voice.
It was Mr Trotsky. 'I dropped it when I was
hiding all the carrots in the forest. The sparkle
spiders must have carried it back to their nest.'

Mira stared at him in surprise. 'But I thought . . .' she said. 'It had an "X" on it and everything . . .'

'Yes, those are my initials,' said the teacher. 'Xavier Trotsky.'

Once Mr Trotsky had led them back to the trail (he was only a *bit* cross about them wandering off it), Dave whizzed around, sniffing out carrots and doing poos in their places. Mira was proud of her unicorn, but most of all she was enjoying being on the trail with all her friends, especially now she'd told them about the treasure egg!

She still wished that she'd been able to *find* some treasure though. She and Jake were the only ones who hadn't put anything in the treasure basket! Raheem had tried to get her to put the egg and the riddle in the basket, but Mira felt silly doing that when she hadn't solved it.

'I'd have been able to solve the treasure-egg mystery if I hadn't had to pick up all this poo,' said Jake. 'Princess and Firework did eight poos between them just now, taking turns.'

'Maybe the treasure is so old it's not even there any more,' said Darcy thoughtfully. 'The writing on the riddle was really curly like in the olden days. Like from when

Miss Glitterhorn learned to write.'

'Maybe you'll both find some treasure at the party,' said Flo. 'You still have loads of time. Mr Trotsky says the party goes on all afternoon until sunset. So in Longest Day time, that's probably a few weeks.'

'No, it's not,' said Raheem.

The trail led them out of the other side of the Fearsome Forest and over a bridge across the Sparkling Stream. As some more trees came into view, they knew where the trail was taking them.

'The GLITTER GLADE!' cheered Class Red.

The Glitter Glade was a field surrounded by

trees, but instead of normal grass the grass was glittery. It was one of the most magical places at Unicorn School.

Dave found the last carrot on the edge of the trees and Mr Trotsky gave them the last purple glittery box. Freya popped it open. Inside was a small bottle of milk.

'A blanket, seeds and milk,' said Darcy, looking through the treasure basket. 'Teachers' idea of treasure is so weird.'

Mira looked up. Sparkling bunting criss-crossed the trees. Colourful pastel Easter egg lanterns shone along the path to the Glitter Glade. All the trees and bushes were flowering. It was like a spring rainbow had exploded all

over the forest. They could hear music and smell delicious party food.

Just where the trees parted into the Glitter Glade itself, Mira saw a huge banner reading 'LONGEST DAY OF THE YEAR!' As Class Red arrived, a massive cheer went up from everyone inside.

'Oh, you made it, we were so worried,' said Miss Glitterhorn, rushing to greet her class.

'Yes, I was really worried about you,' said Miss Hind, holding a plate piled high with glitter-frosted treats.

Rani appeared at the glade entrance. 'Yeah, even I was a bit worried,' she said.

'Really?' asked Mira, nudging Dave to trot

over to her big sister for a hug.

'Urgh, no. Not really. Anyway, there aren't any cupcakes left,' said Rani, wiping her hug off.

'Well, you're here now!' said Miss Glitterhorn. 'Congratulations on completing your Longest Day of the Year activities in the slowest time ever.'

'Woohoo!' Flo punched the air.

'Now, do you have your purple glittery box items?' said Miss Glitterhorn.

'Yes,' said Darcy. 'We tried to swap them for something better but unfortunately had no luck.'

'Well, it's time for your Longest Day

Surprise!' said the teacher.

Class Red all looked at each other. They had thought the party WAS the surprise!

But as Miss Glitterhorn led them into the middle of the Glitter Glade, they realised something EVEN more exciting. There was a little van, with a rainbow and the letters BARCC on the side.

'Baby Animal Rainbow Care Centre!' yelled Flo.

Around the van were some hay bales, where children from other classes were sitting and petting baby animals. There were baby goaticorns, chickicorns and little lambicorns – and even some baby slothicorns!

Flo fainted with happiness.

'So the seeds are for the chickicorns and the milk is for the lambicorns,' said Freya. 'But what about the little blanket?'

'Yeah, I don't see any flying hamsters,' said Seb suspiciously.

'Look over there!' said Tamsin.

On a few of the hay bales, Class Yellow were cuddling tiny pigglicorns wrapped in blankets. The pigglicorns snuffled and grunted and snoozed happily.

Flo sat up. 'This is the best day of my life!' she said and fainted again.

They all filled their plates with treats. Dave did his happy bum-wiggle dance all around

the Glitter Glade and everyone joined in.
As soon as they'd eaten, they queued up to
pet the baby animals.

A while later, Mira was lying in the grass
making glitter angels with Darcy and
Raheem and their unicorns while they waited
for another turn with the baby animals. Dave
was having a food nap. The sun was lower in
the sky now. It glinted through the trees and
on to the glittery grass, making it glow. Mira
felt like she was surrounded by sparkles.

Suddenly she sat up. '*Sparkles galore!*' she said.
'And the grass is *green all around*. And the glade
has four . . . corners? Maybe the treasure is here?'

Mira's chest fizzled with excitement. Maybe

the treasure would be something she could
give her team as a present?

'We'll come look with you!' said Raheem.

'But you'll lose your places in the baby-
animal queue!' said Mira.

'We've got loads of time!' said Tamsin.
'Sunset isn't for hours.'

'Yeah, I could do with a break. I've been
waiting on this pigglicorn for ages,' said
Darcy. 'That boy from Class Blue is hogging
it.' She narrowed her eyes at the hay bales.
The boy from Class Blue hugged the
pigglicorn closer.

'Don't forget your poo collector!' said Jake.

Class Red and their UBFFs raced to each

corner of the Glitter Glade. Jake taught
everyone the treasure hunting walk and soon
they were all doing it, except Dave, who was
still very sleepy from his nap and trying to
hitch a lift on the poo cart. In one corner they
made a human pyramid to look for treasure
up in a tree. In another they hunted in a
hedge, which turned into a big game of hide
and seek. In the next one they got completely
distracted when Seb suggested a game of
Throw the Doughnut on the Unicorn Horn
and Dave was suddenly a lot more alert. By
the time they checked the last corner and
Class Yellow invited them to join a nerf-gun
game, most of them had forgotten what they

were looking for.

'Treasure hunting is the BEST!' said Seb and
Tamsin as they all did the treasure hunting
walk back to the middle of the Glitter Glade.

Mira felt a happy glow. She hadn't found
her treasure, or been crowned Queen Mira,
but treasure hunting was pretty awesome.

Mira was just getting Dave an iced bun
when she saw Jake pushing the poo cart.
She felt bad that he hadn't been able to find
any treasure either. She knew how much
he wanted to be Treasure-Hunt Champion.
Maybe even more than she did!

'Do you want us to do the poo collecting
so you can enjoy the party?' she said.

Jake shook his head. 'You probably won't do it right,' he said. 'Adding the baby animals to the mix has just made the poo levels explode.' He scooped up a poo from behind Sparkles. 'At least most of the unicorns have tiny sparkly number twos.'

He tipped the poo into the poo cart.

Mira stared at the cart.

Sheltered and hidden with sparkles galore,

I'm number two, not one, three or four

Green all around and inside the box,

Is the one special treasure – X marks the spot!

'What?' said Jake.

'THAT'S IT!' said Mira. 'Sparkly poos
– sparkles – *sparkles galore*. The poo cart is
green all around. It has a face with crossed out
eyes on it, like Xs. Number twos are poos –
NUMBER TWOS ARE POOS!' she yelled
and jumped into the air.

'That's nice dear,' said Miss Ponytail,
walking past and looking startled.

'What are you talking about?' said Jake,
looking alarmed.

'THE TREASURE IS IN THE POO
CART!' said Mira.

Jake opened up the poo cart and they
peered inside. It was completely full, so they

had to take out the poo. Eventually Mira could climb in. In one of the sides of the cart was a little hatch. Mira popped it open and there was . . . a treasure chest!

Mira pulled the treasure chest out. It was quite small and not very heavy. She lifted it up in the air. 'I did it! I found the treasure!'

THE POO CART

Jake looked down at the floor. 'Well done,' he said quietly. 'Really good treasure hunting.'

'You helped me find this, though!' Mira said.

Jake frowned. 'No, I didn't. It was right here the whole time and I didn't know.'

'But that's exactly where you said it would be, remember?' said Mira. 'You told me to think *inside the box*, and that it would be under our noses! And then you said "number two!" just now.'

Jake's expression brightened. 'And I taught you the treasure hunting walk!' he said.

'Exactly!' said Mira. She put the box down on the ground and Dave snuffled hopefully around it in case it was edible.

'So it's a bit like the treasure is half mine?' said Jake excitedly.

'Yeah,' said Mira. Jake looked so happy she didn't mind about sharing the treasure hunting glory.

'You might even say it was seventy-five per cent mine and twenty-five per cent yours?' said Jake.

'No, just half,' said Mira.

'Okay, deal,' said Jake. 'Shall we open it?'

'I've got an even better idea!' said Mira.

The sun had got lower and the party was still going on. It really was the Longest Day of the

Year! After all the food and the excitement of cuddling the baby animals everyone was starting to feel sleepy, but they all agreed that it was the best party ever.

Mira and Jake had been busy preparing their special surprise. They had nearly finished when they heard Madame Shetland calling everyone together to look at all the treasure. All the classes' treasure baskets were collected in the middle of the glade and all the children gathered round.

'Quick!' said Mira to Jake and they hurried over.

'Are we all here?' said Madame Shetland. 'Darcy, put that pigglicorn back please. Now,

I must say that this year's haul of treasure is truly wonderful. I think it's the best I've ever seen!'

Mira and Jake reached the back of the group. Mira was out of breath from running.

'We've had wonders of nature,' Madame Shetland continued, holding up Raheem's bag of rocks. 'Amazing inventions and – DARCY! I said, put the pigglicorn back!'

'Oh, I thought you said to put it in my bag,' said Darcy. The pigglicorn poked its face

out of her rucksack and grunted.

Madame Shetland carried on. 'Some of you created artwork, like the Class Blue joint mural of the Crystal Maze Mine. And some of you discovered new skills, like Rhodri and Wizard in Class Indigo, who accidentally learned to surf in the float exercise. And –'

'Ahem,' coughed Flo.

'And one of you even found a ghost. Apparently,' said Madame Shetland.

Flo grinned and gave Gregory a thumbs up.

'So the judges were all in agreement that we couldn't possibly choose just one Treasure-Hunt Champion this year. You are all champions!'

Everyone cheered.

'But we do have a special mention,' said Miss Glitterhorn. 'Jake and Pegasus —'

'Huh?' said Jake, looking up in surprise.

'You collected the most amount of poo we've ever seen,' said Miss Glitterhorn. 'For the Unicorn School gardens, it is a real treasure trove! So we're awarding you this very special badge.'

Jake and Pegasus came forward, still pulling the poo cart behind them. Miss Glitterhorn handed them both gold badges saying *Poo Collector Extraordinaire*. Everyone clapped and cheered, and Class Red cheered the loudest. Jake beamed and Pegasus took a bow.

'I can't wait to tell my dad!' said Jake.

'So I think we have about an hour left before sunset,' said Madame Shetland. 'And the Longest Day comes to an end for this year.'

'Nooooooooooo!' said everyone.

'Madame Shetland?' said Mira, putting up her hand. 'Jake and I have one more bit of treasure if that's okay?'

'Of course, Mira!' said Madame Shetland.

Mira and Dave joined Jake and Pegasus in the centre of the Glitter Glade. She held up her hand. Inside was the plastic egg.

'Ooh, did you solve the treasure-egg mystery?' said Freya.

'Sort of!' said Mira, with a grin. She popped the egg open. Inside there was a new piece of paper, where Mira had written: *Clue One*.

'We hid the treasure again and made a new treasure hunt for everyone!' said Jake.

'Because we realised that searching for the treasure is the most fun part!' said Mira.

The classes cheered and unicorns clapped their hooves.

'All the hard clues are my ones!' said Jake.

So for the last hour of the Longest Day, all the Unicorn School classes did Mira and Jake's treasure hunt. Whenever they found the treasure chest, someone else would hide it in a new place and make up a clue. By the time

the sun had almost set they decided that they would hide the treasure one last time – and then bury a riddle in the egg, so that someone in the future could find it and have their own treasure-egg mystery! They only realised as they were walking back towards Unicorn School that they hadn't even looked inside the treasure chest. They'd been too busy treasure hunting!

'The Longest Day of the Year has been awesome, Dave!' said Mira with a yawn as she and her UBFF trotted along the path. The sun had nearly gone now and was just a glimmer of orange on the horizon. Some of the children had fallen asleep on their unicorns' backs.

Dave looked back at her and burped. A piece of gold foil flew out of his mouth and fluttered to the ground. Mira picked it up. It was the wrapper from a chocolate coin.

She hadn't seen anyone eating chocolate coins . . .

Mira looked over at Dave.

'Did you open the treasure chest and eat the treasure?' she said. Dave burped again.

'And did you replace it with a poo, like you did with the carrots?'

Dave did a proud fart.

Mira grinned. The future treasure hunters were certainly in for a surprise!

Catch up on ALL of Mira and Dave's Adventures at Unicorn School!

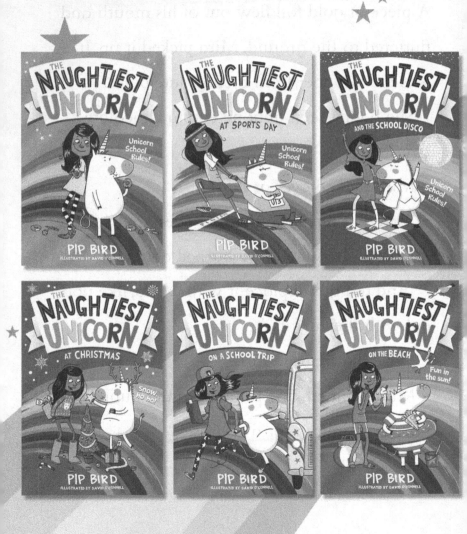

Look out for more magical adventures in *The Naughtiest Unicorn and the Firework Festival*, coming soon!